U0017544

安德魯‧克萊門斯

我是傑克，
霸凌終結者

文◎安德魯‧克萊門斯
譯◎黃筱茵　圖◎唐唐

國家圖書館出版品預行編目（CIP）資料

我是傑克,霸凌終結者 / 安德魯.克萊門斯(Andrew
　Clements)文; 黃筱茵譯; 唐唐圖. --初版. --臺北市:
　遠流, 2013.11
　　面;　公分. -- (安德魯.克萊門斯;13)
　　譯自 : Jake Drake, bully buster
　　ISBN 978-957-32-7298-4（平裝附光碟片）

874.59　　　　　　　　　　　　102020704

安德魯‧克萊門斯13

我是傑克，霸凌終結者

文 / 安德魯‧克萊門斯　譯 / 黃筱茵　圖 / 唐唐

主編 / 林孜憨　內頁設計 / 邱銳致　編輯協力 / 陳懿文
行銷企劃 / 陳佳美　出版一部總編輯暨總監 / 王明雪

發行人 / 王榮文
出版發行 / 遠流出版事業股份有限公司　104005台北市中山北路一段11號13樓
電話：(02)2571-0297　傳真：(02)2571-0197　郵撥：0189456-1
著作權顧問 / 蕭雄淋律師
輸出印刷 / 中原造像股份有限公司
□ 2013年11月1日　初版一刷　　□ 2023年8月25日　初版十五刷

定價 / 新台幣260元 (缺頁或破損的書，請寄回更換)
有著作權‧侵害必究　Printed in Taiwan
ISBN　978-957-32-7298-4
　遠流博識網 http://www.ylib.com　E-mail:ylib@ylib.com
遠流YA讀報粉絲團 https://www.facebook.com/yaread

進入兒童的大人世界

實踐大學應外系講座教授
陳超明

在《傑克與魔豆》的童話故事中，聰明伶俐的傑克（Jack），運用智慧，巧奪巨人的財富；而在現今的校園裡，不同的傑克（Jake），也面臨不一樣的巨人，正要開始現實生活的冒險之旅。

當自己故事的主人翁

每個人小時候，大都擁有聽大人說故事或自己讀故事的喜悅！沉浸在故事的幻想世界裡，不管是小飛俠彼得潘在森林飛舞，還是孫悟空作弄不同妖魔鬼怪，或傑克與巨人間的最後對抗，我們小小的心靈，都暫時脫離父母的嘮叨、學校作業的負擔、隔壁小胖的霸凌，愉快的當自己的主人翁。

從另一面看事情，問題就解決了

　　故事永遠是我們心靈的好夥伴；好的故事，更是我們展現想像力的好場所！將故事結合現實面，這套【我是傑克】系列，帶我們進入「兒童的大人世界」。我們跟隨著主人翁傑克，有如巨人世界的傑克般，進入各種學校與生活冒險。聰明善良的傑克不斷摸索，發掘事情的另一面，找到破解的方法。

　　大家常常說，小孩是個無憂無慮的天使。真的是如此嗎？這些故事顛覆了我們大人的看法。回想一下，我們小時候在學校裡，是不是也要面對很多成長的挑戰：不同階段的霸凌、太聰明或太愚蠢的煩惱、同學老師的排擠或另眼相看？故事裡，傑克願意面對自己的問題，也認識自己有限的能力。故事中常不經意的批評大人的輕忽與便宜行事，往往成為小孩世界的夢魘。

迷人的說故事能力

作者是個說故事高手，以第一人稱的敘述觀點進入小孩的世界，勾劃出這些學校的夢魘，更製造層層高潮，吸引我們閱讀：傑克如何打敗超級霸凌者？傑克如何對抗「師寶」的封號？傑克如何鍛鍊自己的智力？傑克又如何發現老師的另一面？小孩的「成熟」，對照大人的「無知」，正是這些故事迷人的地方。誠如傑克自己所說，他一直搞不懂，學校這些每天在教導他們的大人不是應該很聰明、很厲害嗎？為什麼他們始終沒辦法解決校園霸凌的問題呢？不管是大人，還是小孩，來閱讀這些小孩或大人間的精采互動，都會覺得非常有趣！

如何閱讀本系列作品

【我是傑克】不僅是教導小孩如何找到解決問題的方法，更是

學習語言的好故事書。作者簡潔的語言與故事間的精采轉折，都是本書成功的地方。遠流出版，保留其英文原文，是個非常聰明的作法。我們可以閱讀中文，了解故事情節，也可以回頭看英文，品味這些簡潔語言帶來的美感與魅力。例如 "I tried to smile and nod at him, but I know I looked kind of spooked, because I was spooked. And Link could see I was spooked. And he liked it. And that's when I knew I was in big bully-trouble." 短短四句，重複 spooked，一方面交待傑克成為霸凌對象的過程，一方面也點出其內心的驚慌。這種精采句子到處可見，值得細讀。

這是一系列情節緊湊、語言簡潔、啟發性強的少年故事，大人、小孩都可一起閱讀，不但可以幫助你學習語言，也可以協助你好好面對問題、解決問題！

給讀【我是傑克】的你們

兒童文學作家
幸佳慧

親愛的，我猜，你拿到這本書，可能是父母長輩買來或找來給你的，也可能是同學推薦的。不管怎樣，我們因此在這裡、這一頁相遇。你正讀著字，讀著我這個推薦導讀人寫的字……我的工作就是好好的向你介紹這系列的四本書，就像你的一個好朋友發現了好東西時，會急著和你分享一樣。

安德魯・克萊門斯是美國一位擅長寫學校故事的作家，他總能以學生觀點捉摸到學校生活的各種面相，所以他寫的故事在美國很受歡迎。因為小讀者不會覺得作家藉機說道理（我完全可以體會你們聽說教故事的心情，那感覺就像一朵花好端端的被強行帶到沙漠裡一樣，令人煎熬難受），而是懂得你們的處境或心理，隨著你們

的眼睛去感受學校會發生的事情。那種感覺，就像作家透過文字的魔法讓你們變成一尾尾小魚，跳入小溪、滑入大海去自在悠游，卻同時能帶領你們看到特別的新景物。

【我是傑克】這系列講的是一個小男生在他小學不同年級所發生的故事，每本書就像一片片不同的海域，讓小魚兒帶著熟悉的安全感與新鮮的好奇心去探索。

《我是傑克，霸凌終結者》是在說鎮上新來的一個小惡霸，而且他偏偏挑中傑克當他欺負的對象。這讓傑克有機會回想自己為何老是成為惡霸磁鐵的原因，並且激起他要當霸凌終結者的鬥志。不知道你有沒有被霸凌或霸凌別人的經驗？我幼稚園時，有好幾次被霸凌的經驗，那種恐怖心情，一直到現在還記著呢。你們呢？有思考過為何會發生霸凌，發生了要怎麼應對嗎？

8

《我是傑克，完美馬屁精》這本也是說著我們都熟悉的情境。

我自己就學期間，從幼稚園到博士班都不喜歡那種會巴結老師或討老師歡心的學生，也就是老師眼中的寵物，同學眼中的馬屁精。不過，有時候你偏偏就會被某個老師盯上，他會對你很好，開口閉口都是你，這讓你很困擾，因為你不想被老師馴服、被同學排擠，你想和同學們同一國，卻不知道該怎麼辦？喔，相信我，那可沒那麼簡單，絕對比把期末考考好還要難，但卻有意思極了！

另外，你有沒有過這種經驗？眼前有個大賽，比的正是你的長項，而且獎品非常非常吸引你，為了得獎，你於是進入了一種六親不認、全力以赴，卻又疑神疑鬼的狀態。整個過程很煎熬，考驗著你和家人、同學的關係，也衝擊著自己對自己的信心，但同時一路上也可能出現意外而有趣的路口，等著你轉彎過去！如果有，那你

一定要讀《我是傑克，超跩萬事通》這一本。

另一本《我是傑克，天才搞笑王》也描述了我小時候在學校經歷過的事，就是你明明知道在老師面前「乖乖的」便可以沒事，但你還是忍不住「搞怪」。你也知道下一刻因此要惹禍上身，卻意外觀察到老師們有異狀，然後你才慢慢發現，其實他們有另一個不是老師的身份存在。這個新發現讓你重新看待自己和大人的關係，也才知道原來上學這件事有好笑、溫柔與不為人知的一面呢！

總之，我很努力的向你們介紹這四本書有意思且吸引人的地方，希望你接下去有機會翻完它們，並回過頭來評評我分享的話有沒有道理。若覺得沒道理，那也很好，這樣你就可以開始寫你想分享給其他小讀者的推薦導讀了，我可是很樂意拜讀的！

名家好評推薦

乖巧、伶俐，帶著一點膽怯，卻又總是強自鎮定的傑克，和我兒子正好同年，今年十歲，四年級。而且，有點小聰明的性格也有那麼一點類似呢！所以，每當我看到傑克在學校裡遇到麻煩與困擾時，忍不住也會想像，當我兒子遇到同樣情形時，他會怎麼辦？

克萊門斯的作品活潑逗趣，貼近小朋友的想法與經歷，讀來輕鬆愉快，又引人入勝。【我是傑克】系列以中英雙語方式出版，拉長了閱讀年齡層，讓高年級的孩子也可以把它當成一本練習英文的讀本，是相當值得收藏的好書喔！

——親子作家　陳安儀

11

1 惡霸磁鐵

我是傑克，全名叫傑克·德瑞克，今年四年級；到目前為止，這是我最棒的一個年級。今年我的導師是男老師──湯普森先生。他滿老的，可是不兇。今年和我喜歡同一類的書，像是關於火山、叢林與海洋的書，還有冒險故事、笑話集、《凱文與跳跳虎》漫畫之類的東西。

不過，關於湯普森先生，有一件事情很奇怪。皮特是第

一個發現的人。這很合理，因為皮特是個喜歡科學的小孩，他會收集昆蟲、化石、植物，還知道這些東西的名字。他也許是全校最聰明的小孩。

開學大約兩個星期後，皮特指著湯普森先生，然後小聲的說：「他又穿那種長褲了。」

「什麼長褲？」我說。

「那種長褲呀，」皮特說：「他昨天、前天、大前天都穿同樣的長褲。我想他一定是每天都穿同一件長褲。」

「不會吧，」我說：「他可能有很多件一樣的長褲啦，就是那樣。」

所以皮特說：「我要來測試我的理論。」

知道我的意思了吧？喜歡科學的小孩就是這樣。

那天下午，我們的朗讀時間在地毯上進行，湯普森先生坐在一張懶骨頭椅上，皮特就坐在湯普森先生的斜後方。湯普森先生開始朗讀瑞士的羅賓森一家人的故事，正讀到他們的船撞毀的那一段。

班上同學有些人看著湯普森先生的臉，有些人看著天花板或其他地方，而我那時候正看著皮特。

皮特的手從口袋裡伸出來，在湯普森先生腳後停留一下，接著又回到他的口袋裡。然後皮特坐下來，像其他人一樣聽講。

朗讀時間結束時，我跑到皮特旁邊小聲的說：「你做了

什麼？」

皮特咧著嘴笑，從口袋裡掏出一個東西。是一枝小小的黑色奇異筆，顏色洗不掉的那種。

我跑到湯普森先生背後往下一看，在他右腳褲管底下褶邊的後面，有一個很小的黑點。

我們就是那樣發現湯普森先生真的有兩件長褲。每個星期四，他都會穿上和另一件長褲一模一樣的黃褐色長褲，只是這一件上面沒有那個小黑點，看起來也比較新。皮特的理論是：湯普森先生他們家一定是在星期四洗衣服；因為每到星期五，我們都會再看見那個小小的點。

我最好的朋友是菲爾‧威利斯，大家都叫他威利，他今年和我不同班。我們會一起上體育、音樂和美術課，不過其他時間，威利都在史提爾太太班上。我真慶幸我的導師是湯普森先生。我是說，史提爾太太還不錯啦，但是威利的功課比我多很多，況且史提爾太太還是個拼字狂、數學狂，還有社會課狂……我猜她對任何事物都很狂熱吧。所以呢，威利這一年最愛上的是體育課。

就像我剛才說的，我現在念四年級，也就是說，到目前為止我已經上學五年了。如果把我去「露露小姐點心尿布托嬰中心」那兩年和托兒所那一年都加上去的話，差不多有八年。我上學八年了。

我是傑克，霸凌終結者

接下來就是我搞不懂的地方啦。如果在學校工作的每個大人都那麼聰明，他們怎麼沒辦法解決霸凌事件呢？為什麼只要遇到霸凌的問題，小孩就得靠自己？

因為每一年都發生一樣的事，霸凌。

我來解釋一下好了。好吧，這要說到我三歲在露露小姐托嬰中心那時候。我才去第二天，上午過了一半，在我排隊領牛奶和餅乾的時候，有一個流著鼻涕、穿著寬鬆吊帶褲的小孩直接插隊在我前面。

我一句話都沒說，因為不知道該怎麼辦。記得嗎？我那時候才三歲，我還以為是流鼻涕的小孩可以排在前面。

於是我拿了我的餅乾和牛奶坐到桌子前。鼻涕男孩坐在

20

我對面。我對他笑一笑，喝一口我的牛奶。

那他做了什麼？他把手伸過來，拿走我的兩片餅乾。我連牛奶還來不及吞下去，他就把兩片餅乾各咬了一大口，上面沾滿口水。然後他把餅乾放回我的餐巾上，對著我笑。

我看著從他鼻子裡跑出來的東西，再看看我的餅乾，轉頭找露露小姐。

她還在發點心。這裡有人做了壞事了，但露露小姐在忙。

所以我很快的把手伸出去，拿走**他的**餅乾。但我低頭一看，發現鼻涕男孩早就咬過他的餅乾了。

他又笑了，我可以看到他牙齒上黏著餅乾屑和巧克力片。於是我告訴自己：「誰要吃點心啊？」我把他的餅乾輕

輕放回桌子對面，喝掉我剩下的牛奶之後，就到外面玩。

三分鐘後，我在盪鞦韆上，試著讓鞦韆動起來。可是有人抓住鞦韆的鍊子。沒錯，又是那個鼻涕男孩。

他吸了一下鼻子說：「我的。」鼻涕男孩不太會講話。

而我大概是回答他說：「我先來的。」這是個錯誤。對付惡霸的第一個原則就是：不要試著和他說他哪裡有錯，惡霸不喜歡聽。

他把鍊子用力一拽，說：「不！我的！」

我看看四周，露露小姐在遊戲場另一邊。鼻涕男孩又用力扯了一下鍊子，我只好從鞦韆上下來。

鼻涕男孩是我遇過的第一個惡霸。接下來四年，我就是

一個惡霸磁鐵。

在托兒所的時候是麥克‧拉達，我都叫他破壞狂。管他是積木、樂高玩具、冰棒棍、蠟筆，還是紙，無論我做了什麼東西，也不管這東西是用什麼做的，破壞狂都會把它撕成碎片。

幼稚園的時候是肯尼‧羅素，他是撞人王。每天都被撞或被推很多次，真的很糟。好比你站在公車站牌邊，身旁有一灘水，或是你正在喝一盒巧克力牛奶，或是你正在畫畫，只要有機會撞人，撞人王就在那裡，整個幼稚園時期都這樣。

到了一年級，我遇到的主要惡霸是傑克‧勒納，大家都叫他「拳頭」。傑克從來沒有真的揍過我，只是打我旁邊的東

西，像是便當袋，幾乎每天都這樣。一個大拳頭對一個美而美三明治做了很糟糕的事。我很快就學到，不要帶任何小盒布丁去上學。整個一年級期間，我都吃餅乾屑當點心。

那就是我，傑克·德瑞克，惡霸磁鐵，就好像是所有惡霸都聚在一起挑選他們最喜歡的目標。方圓幾里內的每個惡霸好像都知道我是他們最好下手的完美小孩。我想，我終於知道他們為什麼這麼喜歡我了。

其中一個原因是：惡霸需要找一個身材中等的小孩。如果這個小孩太壯，那麼他們總有一天會打起來。惡霸並不喜歡打架。但是如果這個小孩太弱小，霸凌別人就會變得太容易、太沒有挑戰性。

惡霸喜歡我的另一個原因是因為我沒有哥哥，甚至連姊姊都沒有。我只有艾比，她比我小兩歲。惡霸馬上就會看出這種事。

惡霸還看得出來我不是那種一有問題就會跑去報告老師的小孩。老是唉唉叫的告狀鬼對惡霸來說是很差勁的誘餌。

而且，我想我看起來滿有頭腦的。大部分的惡霸好像都不是那麼聰明，當他們看到一個好像滿有頭腦的小孩時，身體裡就會有個聲音說：「噢，是嗎？現在看看你要怎麼應付

我，聰明的傢伙！」

我猜我是個聰明的傢伙，因為思考是我很拿手的事。就因為我很會思考，我終於學會該怎麼對付惡霸。不過我並不

是立刻想通所有的事。想這些事花了我漫長的四年，就在我

一一對付了鼻涕男孩、破壞狂、撞人王，還有拳頭以後。

我還得先被一個不折不扣、最強的超級霸凌王盯上。那

是在我二年級的時候發生的事，我也是在那一年變成了霸凌

終結者——傑克·德瑞克。

2 超級霸凌王

二年級一開始就很棒。爸媽設法讓我編進布萊托太太的班級。他們告訴我，她是戴普雷小學最好的老師。她常常微笑，不會出回家作業，教室裡的東西都安排得整整齊齊，所以我很高興她是我的老師。

菲爾・威利斯的老師也是布萊托太太。威利和我二年級的時候就已經是最好的朋友了，我們每天都玩得很開心。我

們坐在同一組，還是閱讀夥伴。我們每天都一起吃午餐，休息時間總是一起混。我們搭的不是同一班公車，不過有時放學後我會去他家，有時他會來我家。

最棒的是，布萊托太太班上沒有惡霸，連半個都沒有，真是太棒了。在午餐時間和去遊戲場玩的時候，我還是要小心，不過大部分時候，我的生活都可以不受惡霸騷擾。

然而，就在萬聖節前，有個新來的小孩搬到鎮上。他一走進布萊托太太的教室，我就知道我有麻煩了。

布萊托太太說：「孩子們，我們今天有一位新同學，他的名字叫林克‧貝柯斯特。」

她繼續介紹，不過我們全都看著那個新來的小孩。對二

年級的人來說，他長得有點高。他一頭金髮，鼻子很尖，手臂很長，手掌很大。

林克‧貝柯斯特站在那兒，也開始看著我們教室裡所有的人。他看到我的時候停了下來。我仔細看著他的臉，發現林克‧貝柯斯特有著又圓又亮的小眼睛，那是惡霸的眼睛。

林克看到我發現這一點了，接著，他對我微笑。

那不是善良的微笑。

那麼，布萊托太太呢？這位女士應該是超棒的老師吧？

她做了什麼呢？她把林克編進我和威利這一組！

威利馬上就小聲對他說：「嗨，我叫菲爾，但其實我是威利。威利是我的小名。」

你知道了吧，威利從來沒有遇過霸凌的問題，主要是因為他的個子太小了。他是個好孩子，他管好自己的事，惡霸似乎甚至不會注意到他。

所以林克對威利微笑，跟他說：「嗨！」

然後威利指著我說：「他是傑克。」

林克·貝柯斯特用他又圓又亮的小眼睛盯著我，再次露出那種惡霸的笑容，然後說：「傑克。好吧。」

我試著對他點頭微笑，可是我知道我看起來有點像見到鬼，因為我真的是見鬼了。林克看得出我見鬼的表情，他很得意，而我就是那個時候知道自己在霸凌這件事上遇到了天大的麻煩。

林克只有八歲，和我一樣，但我從一開始就看得出他有大計畫。他想當霸凌者明星隊裡的最有價值隊員，他想登上霸凌者名人堂。而我，傑克·德瑞克，我就是他的新計畫。

林克到班上的第一天，我們在練習寫字。布萊托太太發下來一些畫了線的白紙，我們必須非常、非常整齊的寫下六個句子。只有在練習寫字的時後，我們才能用原子筆，而不是用鉛筆。

我好愛用我的原子筆。它是用亮紅色塑膠做的，有黑色的墨水。原子筆旁邊有一個按鍵，當我按下按鍵，它就會發出喀的一聲，頂端會彈起來。

我的第五個句子正寫到一半，快要寫好了。我的原子筆

滑過平順的紙，寫好的句子看起來很棒。

然後林克很快的搖了一下他的桌子。我的桌子接在他的桌子旁邊，所以我的原子筆突然抖得一塌糊塗。我的紙看起來亂七八糟。

我抬起頭看著林克，他笑了，接著小聲對我說：「筆不賴唷。」

我去找布萊托太太要一張新的紙，重新抄了一次句子，可是這一次我從頭到尾一直看著林克，好確定他不會再搖晃他的桌子。我緊張得不得了，害自己又寫壞了兩張紙，而林克沒有任何動作。

我讓自己鎮定下來，已經寫到最後一個句子。布萊托太

太在教室後面幫一個小孩的忙。林克很快伸手過來，輕輕彈我的耳朵。雖然不是很大力，卻剛好讓我跳了一下。我的筆滑掉了，紙上再次變得亂糟糟。

你懂了吧，林克不是個普通的惡霸。任何大塊頭的小孩去使喚個子小的小孩，那是一種霸凌，但是現在情況不同。林克‧貝柯斯特，嗯……他才花二十分鐘就完全占據了我的腦袋。不用說，這個惡霸真的很有天分。

這就是我遇到的狀況。我向布萊托太太要第五張紙，她說：「傑克，你應該更小心一點。」

我差點要大喊出來：「是啊，嘿，是**你**應該更小心一點。你難道不知道你的班上有一個超級霸凌者嗎？」

可是我當然沒有那樣說。因為惡霸的第二項原則就是，如果你去向老師告狀，事情就會變得更糟。而且我有一種預感，事情會比現在的狀況還要糟。

我的預感沒錯。

3 比糟糕還糟

在林克第一天上學結束後，我搭上公車。我望向窗外，看見林克走在布萊托太太身後。她正指給他看要搭哪一班公車回家。

「拜託，」我低聲說：「不要和我同一車，不要是三號車。拜託、拜託、拜託，不要是三號公車。」

不過，布萊托太太就直接帶他走到三號公車這裡。十秒

鐘後，林克就在我坐的這輛車上，站在我旁邊，低頭看著我。

他用遠比必要的音量大很多的聲音說：「嘿，肥克，這裡有人坐嗎？」

我向上看，想起他有多高了。而這時他正用我的名字搞怪。他已經讓我同時感到火大又害怕，可是我不在乎，因為我不想他拿我的名字開玩笑。

所以我說：「我的名字叫傑克，傑克‧德瑞克。」我馬上就知道自己做錯了，因為現在他知道我很在意他拿我的名字亂扯這件事。

林克露出惡霸那種特別的微笑。他說：「是啊，我知道啊。就像我說的，你的名字叫做肥克，肥克‧德瑞克。」他的

話讓車上其他小孩笑了，然後他就在我旁邊坐下來。

他沒有推我或揍我，因為任何人都可以做那種事。他用的是新的霸凌方式，他是個超級霸凌者。

我感覺耳朵變紅了，嘴唇抿得很緊。我轉頭望向窗外不看他。我準備好接受下一次攻擊了。

可是攻擊沒有出現。隔著走道的座位上有個四年級生，他有一隻棒球手套。於是林克說：「這個鎮上最棒的小聯盟隊伍是哪一支？」

接著，林克開始講到他以前是如何加入舊家鎮上最棒的那支隊伍。他不想加入新隊伍，除非那支隊伍會是贏家。

他講話的方式好像我不在場。我坐在他的旁邊耶，但我

卻像身在月球一樣。

公車停在楓樹街上，有一些小孩下車。下一站是十字街，更多小孩下車。接著，公車就要到達我下車的那一站——綠林街。

所以我說：「我要在這站下車。」公車慢下來的時候，大概有十個小孩站起來，可是林克還在繼續和那個四年級生聊著小聯盟的事。

所以我更大聲的說：「我到站了，我要在這裡下車。」

我望向前面的座位，公車司機旁邊只剩下三個小孩了。

我大喊：「**現在**。我**現在**就要下車！」

公車司機往上看著她的後照鏡，皺了皺眉頭。可是林克

對她微笑，然後用大到每個人都聽得見的聲音說：「哎呀，肥克，我差點就忘了。記得嗎？我是新來的。我也是到這一站。我和肥克・德瑞克要在這一站下車。」

要我跟著林克・貝柯斯特下車？那是我人生中最糟糕的時刻之一。我走下那些高高的黑色台階時，心想：每個早上、每個下午，還有二年級接下來的每一天（說不定甚至包括我以後的日子），都會是我和林克・貝柯斯特一起。

有些事一定要改變。

4 霸凌者病

我下車的時候，林克甚至沒有和我說話。他就這樣走掉了。我看著他，他穿過了綠林街，開始由公園街往下走。

然後我想起來了。那還用說嗎？林克搬進卡森家的舊房子呀。之前那棟房子要賣，而現在則是林克家的房子了；就在公園街上，在我家路口的轉角。

我走進我家時，甚至沒有和媽媽打招呼。我把書包丟在

地上，然後直接走進遊戲間。

我的妹妹，艾比，正在看布偶演的電視節目。那是她最喜歡的節目。

我說：「那個給我！」然後就從她手中搶走遙控器。她對我皺皺眉，吐吐舌頭。我把電視頻道轉到《蝙蝠俠》。

艾比說：「喂！我正在看我的娃娃耶！」

我說：「喔，是嗎？」然後我走到她旁邊。她坐在地上一個大枕頭上，我感覺比她高了很多。我說：「嘿，我在看《蝙蝠俠》，你又不能拿我怎樣！」接著我踢了她的枕頭。

艾比大喊：「噢！噢！很痛耶！媽，傑克搶人家的遙控器啦！他剛才還踢我，**很用力耶！**」

媽媽進來了。她很快的走來，就是用那種「你完蛋了」的速度。

她停下來，站在我面前說：「傑克‧德瑞克，你應該懂事到不會在這裡胡鬧才對！馬上回廚房把你的書包撿起來，把遙控器還給你妹妹。」

我把遙控器丟給艾比，卻意外打到她的膝蓋。「噢——」

這下子她真的大叫了，而且還試著哭了一下下。

於是我很快的說：「對不起！」但是太遲了。媽媽抓住我的手臂，把我拖到廚房去。

她拉我去坐在一張椅子上，然後說：「傑克，在這個家裡，我們不會那樣對待別人的，這你明明知道啊！你到底是

怎麼回事？」

然後我想到了，是林克，我被林克附身了！我表現得就

像林克那樣。我得了「霸凌者病」！

可是我不能告訴媽媽有關林克的事，因為我媽可能會打

電話給林克的媽媽，然後林克就會對公車上的每個人說肥

克‧德瑞克是怎樣哭著找媽媽；這樣的話，我以後每天搭公

車都會聽到他們說我是個大寶寶。

所以我說：「媽媽，對不起。」接著大大嘆了口氣。「我

想我只是又累又餓。」

媽媽們喜歡聽到這句話。又累又餓，這都是媽媽知道怎

麼樣處理的事。

媽媽拍拍我的頭，給我一個花生醬三明治和一杯牛奶，

然後她說：「寶貝，今天晚上我一定會讓你早早上床睡覺，

但是你吃完那個三明治之後，要去向艾比道歉。」

於是我慢慢的吃，接著把我的盤子和杯子放進水槽，再

去找艾比。

我還以為這一次就和我之前向艾比說對不起的狀況一樣。

可是不一樣。

5 艾比怎麼說

在我上二年級的時候，艾比還在念幼稚園。即使如此，艾比不像很多其他小小孩那麼笨。

我從來沒有告訴過她這一點，不過有時艾比是個可以聊天的對象；你知道的，就一個妹妹來說。我的意思是，因為我沒有養狗或其他動物，所以艾比就像一隻會說話的寵物。有點像鸚鵡啦，我猜。

反正，我對艾比說我很抱歉。

「沒關係。」她說。

關於艾比有多像一隻寵物這點，你懂我的意思了吧？你知道嗎？如果你對一隻狗大叫，牠會很怕你，甚至很氣你；可是你再拍拍牠的頭，牠又會開始對你搖尾巴。艾比就是那個樣子。

她還在看那些布偶。他們正在牆上畫一些雲。真蠢。

我告訴艾比關於林克的事。

艾比說：「他妹妹今天來上學。琳達‧貝柯斯特。她和我一起上幼稚園。她也會欺負別人。」

我說：「真的嗎？」

「對呀，」艾比說：「琳達搶走莎拉的蠟筆，我看到了。」

艾比開始像那些布偶一樣揮動她的手臂。

我說：「所以她搶走了莎拉的蠟筆？」

艾比點點頭，沒有專心聽我說。「對呀。最棒的顏色。琳達說：『如果你敢講出去，我就把這些蠟筆折斷。』到了點心時間，莎拉給琳達一片麗茲餅乾，後來琳達才讓莎拉用那枝黃色的蠟筆。」

就是這樣，蠟筆綁架案。

我心想：琳達‧貝柯斯特才上幼稚園而已！林克的小妹妹已經是個超級霸凌者了。我接著又想：想想看，她的大哥哥會怎麼對付我？

真是個不好的想法。

艾比繼續看布偶秀。節目快結束了，布偶們開始唱歌，節目的這個部分幾乎快讓我吐了。

接著我想起一件事。我想到之前去佛羅里達州探望外公外婆時，只有我和艾比去。那時我很生氣，因為做任何事都得和艾比一起；她才四歲，還在上托兒所，而我已經是一年級的大哥哥了。我討厭自己走到哪裡身邊都跟著一個嬰兒。

我從頭到尾都對艾比很壞。

於是我說：「還記得我們去佛羅里達的時候，我對你有多壞嗎？」

艾比正在配合音樂點頭。可是她說：「我記得。」

y

艾比怎麼說

我說：「你為什麼沒有對我發脾氣？」

艾比聳聳肩。「如果我發脾氣，就會感覺自己很壞，我不想覺得自己很壞，所以我沒有生氣。」

之後艾比開始跟著布偶們一起唱歌。我不想吐出來，所以就回到我的房間，跳到床上，想一想我遇到的問題。

一部分的我希望可以每天早上都搭爸爸的便車上學，這樣就不必和林克一起搭公車，說不定下課時間還可以去圖書館，然後媽媽會來接我放學。

一部分的我希望一個晚上就可以長高二十幾公分，那樣我明天早上就會搭公車，坐在林克旁邊，把他的臉壓在窗戶上。我會用紅色奇異筆畫他的鼻子。我會叫他粉克。粉克‧

貝柯斯特。

但我繼續想。艾比說得沒錯，覺得自己很壞並不有趣。

而林克表現得就像那樣子**很有趣**。可是那樣不好玩，真的。

這樣好玩嗎？不，不可能好玩的。

那天晚上我上床睡覺的時候，這樣告訴我自己：「明天，我不要對林克生氣。不管發生什麼事。那樣他就會明白對別人很壞一點也不好玩。」

這對艾比和我是有效的。

可是對一個超級霸凌者有效嗎？

6 耍酷

到了早上，林克上車後確認一下就坐在我旁邊。首先，他把鞋子上的泥巴掃到我的書包上。但我只是笑一笑，把灰塵撢開。太酷了。

他叫我傑克・肥列克。我笑著說：「對啊，說得好！不然叫我蛇內克・德瑞克怎麼樣？或者是……起司蛋糕・德瑞克？還是……還是叫搖搖傑克？好耶，搖搖傑克。」

公車上的每個人都笑了。不過，是我讓他們笑出來，不是林克。我在耍酷。

林克不喜歡這樣。他圓亮的小眼睛變得愈來愈傷人。我們到學校的時候，他一路推擠到公車最前面，所以是第一個下車。他甚至推擠了一些五年級生。

在班上的情況更糟。林克把一些口香糖黏在我的數學作業簿上。我只是笑了笑，在黏答答的地方貼上一張紙。我繼續做我的事，酷斃了。

上美術課時，林克在我的顏料裡倒了一些金粉。我說：

「好主意！」然後繼續畫圖。

後來，美術老師說：「傑克，我**好愛**你這幅作品，真有

創意。」

真有創意，而且真**酷**。

我很擔心下課時間。遊戲場很大，任何事都可能發生。

可想而知，在溜滑梯的時候，林克插隊排在我後面。我想把他一溜下去，他就在我後面用超級快的速度往下溜。可是我很迅速的站到旁邊，還讓他的腳沾到了一些泥巴。

布萊托太太站得那麼近真是件好事，否則林克可能會試著叫我把泥巴從他的鞋子上舔乾淨，或者做些什麼事。

午餐後，我在男生廁所洗手。我照著鏡子，鏡子裡還有林克，他正對我微笑。我試著回他一個微笑，但是好難啊。

我很害怕。

林克繼續微笑，他開始在我旁邊的水槽洗手。我拿起一張紙巾時，他捧起雙手，朝著我潑灑一堆水，就潑在我黃褐色的長褲前面，有很大一塊溼掉的咖啡色痕跡。

然後林克用一種娃娃音說：「哇！哇！哭哭小傑發生意外了！」一群四年級生開始指指點點還大笑。

我也試著大笑。我試著表現得很酷，可是我沒辦法。我沒辦法笑，沒辦法對這件事笑，我很生氣，我感覺有火要從我的眼睛裡射出來了。

林克看到了。他看到我生氣了，然後他也看出我因為他看到我生氣而更加火大。林克圓亮的小眼睛和他得意的小嘴

笑了起來，在笑我。

我盡量在男生廁所裡待久一點，用紙巾擦拭我的長褲，用手對著長褲搧風。可是回到教室的時候，我的褲子上還是有一大塊深色的汙漬。

林克正在講悄悄話。我進教室時，每個人都看著我。我的臉脹得通紅。當我在林克對面坐下時，他摀住鼻子，做了個鬼臉。

我受不了了。我非常憤怒，那樣讓我覺得自己很壞。我輸了。我轉向林克，用盡力氣痛搥他的肩膀。

我並不是真的很有力氣，所以我知道我沒有真的弄傷他。

但林克比艾比還要會演戲。他抓住自己的肩膀，還把他

桌上的一本書打飛。

「啊！」他大喊：「啊！我的手臂，我的手臂！」

布萊托太太才一秒鐘就過來了。「傑克！你太過分了！」

林克讓他的手臂垂下來，好像斷掉了一樣。他哀嚎著：

「啊！我的手臂，我的手臂！好痛！」

布萊托太太說：「泰德，請幫忙陪林克去保健室。傑克，你跟我來。」

林克離開教室時偷偷回看我一眼。他笑了。

林克‧貝柯斯特離開教室，他去拿一些冰塊，還有接受護士親切的問話。

那我呢？我離開教室去和校長談話，應該不會是愉快的

聊一下，況且我的褲子前面還是留著一塊很大的痕跡。

布萊托太太陪我沿著走廊走。在這段路程中，我想清楚

了一些事情。林克比艾比遇過的任何人都要麻煩。

這是一場戰爭，我輸了。輸得慘兮兮。

這不酷。一點也不酷。

7 學到教訓

當人們對你發脾氣時，他們會一直東指西指。到了辦公室，布萊托太太就指著一張椅子。她說：「在這裡等。」她沒有笑，然後就走進校長的辦公室。

一分鐘後，她出來了，校長卡普太太也出來了。卡普太太指著她的辦公室說：「傑克，進去。」

我以前從沒來過校長辦公室。那裡有一張很大的灰色桌

子，一排很大的灰色書架，還有一個很大的灰色校長。卡普太太穿著灰鞋子、灰洋裝，頭上頂著灰色頭髮。她比布萊托太太高，甚至比我爸還要高。

她指著她桌子前面的一張灰色椅子。「坐那裡，傑克。」那並不是真的在問我問題。

所以我坐了下來。然後她說：「你知道打人是違反規定的，對吧？」

我說：「是的，我知道。」

「那你為什麼要打林克‧貝柯斯特？」

這一部分就很難處理了。如果我把林克欺負人的事說出來，我就成了告狀鬼；可是如果我不說點什麼，校長會認為我是亂打人的瘋子，所以我就指著長褲上的水漬說：「我的

褲子在男生廁所沾到水了，我以為林克在笑我。」

這麼簡單、這麼真實，讓卡普太太很容易了解。而她真的了解了，就像那樣。她的臉上出現一個友善的表情，說：

「傑克，我了解尷尬的感覺。可是你知道無論發生什麼事，打人都是不對的嗎？」

於是我說：「知道。」因為這句話是真的，我真的很抱歉打了林克。我不想和他打架，一點也不想。這有兩個原因：

第一，因為打人、踢人、抓人、拉頭髮、在地上打滾都很不好。第二，因為我知道如果我真的和林克打架會有什麼下場。我會變成好大一塊紫色瘀青。

所以卡普太太讓我回教室，她甚至沒有打電話給我媽。

她幫我打開校長辦公室的門，說：「我相信你一定學到教訓了。對吧，傑克？」

我說：「是的，卡普太太。」只是我不知道我們在講的是不是同樣的教訓。

我從學校辦公室走向布萊托太太的教室，這時林克正好從保健室出來。我覺得他是在等我。他走在我旁邊。在空曠的走道上，林克好像比平常都還要高大。

他給了我那種惡霸的微笑，然後說：「肥列克，做得不錯喔。和校長在一起很開心吧？」

這是我第一次和林克獨處。我很害怕，不過我說：「還不賴啊。」我們繼續走著。

和林克獨處的感覺不太一樣。我以為如果周圍沒有其他小孩在看，惡霸就不會欺負人；我以為要有觀眾在場，才會是個超級霸凌者。有一下下的時間，我覺得林克只不過是一個高大的小孩，而我正和他一同走過走廊。

在那個時候，我對惡霸的認識還沒有現在那麼多。所以我說：「你為什麼找上我？」

我問錯問題了，超級霸凌者回來了。林克看著我，就像我是一隻小蟲似的。他說：「笨蛋問題。」我以為他說不定準備把我推進置物櫃或是做些什麼事。

可是他沒有，我們只是繼續走。

不過我的問題好像讓他很困擾。在我們回到二十三號教

室前，我知道了。我知道他為什麼沒有回答那個問題。

他沒有回答，是因為他**沒辦法**回答。他沒辦法告訴我為

什麼，因為他真的不知道。

但是，林克會變成惡霸一定有個理由。

如果我能找出那個原因（或是我能給他一個**不用**當惡霸

的理由），那麼超級霸凌者林克·貝柯斯特就會變成**前任**霸凌

者林克·貝柯斯特。

8 危險二重奏

下個星期並不好玩。

林克只要一找到機會，就會做一些很壞的事，像是踩在我的紅筆上把紅筆弄斷。有時是做一些讓我出糗的事，像是在餐廳裡把我推向一群四年級女生；有時是做一些惹我生氣的事，像是把我的書包藏在公車最後面的座位底下。

我開始覺得，林克會變惡霸是因為他本來就是惡霸，而

且我開始覺得自己根本沒有辦法改變這種狀況，我只能忍耐下去。每一天。我往後的生活都是如此。

就在我覺得事情不可能更慘的時候，一切變得更糟糕。

這都要感謝布萊托太太。

感恩節快到了，我們每個人必須做一個和感恩節有關的社會科報告。布萊托太太設計好所有主題，她要我們兩個人一組，由布萊托太太決定每一組的成員配對。其中一組就是傑克·德瑞克和林克·貝柯斯特。我們必須做一份報告來告訴大家美洲原住民是如何生活的。

林克超愛這個主意，他覺得這樣很好笑，超大的笑話。

他說：「嘿，肥列克，這太棒了，你和我一組。我們要

一起做一個梯皮帳篷❶。告訴你，我來做『梯』的部分，你來做『皮』的部分。懂了沒？皮蛋？」

其他人都去吃午餐時，我去找布萊托太太。我說：「布萊托太太，我不認為應該和林克一起合作感恩節報告。」

她說：「哦？為什麼呢？」

「嗯，」我說：「我只是覺得和別人同組會表現更好。」

布萊托太太說：「很抱歉，傑克，可是其他人都已經分好組了，我相信你和林克一定會合作得很好的。」

❶ 梯皮帳篷（teepee）是美洲原住民的一種傳統圓錐形帳篷。故事這裡是林克用諧音字在開傑克玩笑，他故意將 teepee 拆開來說，而後者 pee 為「尿尿、撒尿」之意。

那天在回家的公車上，林克說：「那個感恩節什麼的？

肥列克，你要報告，我才不做那種蠢事。」

我說：「你說這話是什麼意思？我們同一組耶。」

林克說：「是呀，對，所以你就是要做報告的那個組員。」

第二天有圖書館時間。我看著林克，他立刻跑去參考書區，拿了字首是N的百科全書。我心想：「太好了，他要去查有關美洲原住民（Native Americans）的資料了。」林克把百科全書拿到圖書館後面一張桌子上。我的組員在工作，看起來狀況不錯。

我去找其他生活在麻薩諸塞州的北美原住民資料。

圖書館時間快結束時，我把我找到的書拿給林克看。

他抬頭說：「做得不賴唷，肥列克。」

我說：「你找到什麼？」

他說：「讓你看看。」在百科全書後面，林克正在看一本《加菲貓》漫畫。他說：「我很喜歡社會課，你也是吧？」

所以情況就是這麼一回事：我的組員不但是個超級霸凌者，還是個笨蛋。

之後，到了提出報告的前一天。

我負責找了全部的書；我負責找了全部的圖片；我用我最工整的字跡寫了一些標籤；我手邊有自己看得懂的資料，

但我們還是沒有任何能給同學看的梯皮帳篷或其他東西。

快放學的時候，布萊托太太說：「記得喔，明天所有人都要交感恩節報告。」

那天下午，我們下了公車之後，林克走到我的旁邊說：

「嘿，肥列克，你做完那份白痴報告了嗎？」

我說：「還沒。我們還要做些東西來展示美洲原住民的生活。」

他說：「這個嘛，你最好今天晚上把它完成。」

就是他說這句話的方式，好像可以隨便命令我一樣。他以為可以只看著我，然後要我去做所有他叫我做的事。可是我受夠了一個人做全部的工作，這樣不公平。

我心裡有什麼東西突然喀嚓斷掉。所以我說：「不，我才不幹。」

林克靠近我一步。他說：「什麼？」

「我說我才不幹，我不在乎你講什麼或你做什麼。如果你不幫忙，我猜我們報告的成績就會不及格。」

林克用他又圓又亮的惡霸小眼睛往下看著我。他握緊拳頭。有一秒鐘的時間，我覺得自己好像犯了大錯，我會被他揍到人行道上。

可是他突然聳聳肩說：「好吧，沒問題。三點半左右來我家，我們來做個愚蠢的梯皮帳篷之類的東西。」

然後他只是轉個身，開始往他家的方向走去。

站在綠林街和公園街的街角，在十一月的陽光下，我覺得好像有什麼改變了，那感覺並不像我剛剛殺了一條龍還是什麼的。

那比較像是回到我五歲的時候，我每天晚上都覺得床底下有一隻怪獸，有一天晚上，我鼓足勇氣往床下看；怪獸不在那裡，沒有怪獸。

但是我四十五分鐘後就要去敲林克家的門了，誰會來開門呢？

會是我社會科報告的組員嗎？

還是一隻怪獸？

9 驚奇與疑問

找到林克的家並不是問題，他就住在吉米・卡森的舊房子裡，我已經去過那裡很多次。我的書包裡裝著報告需要用到的所有資料。

我走上前門階梯按了門鈴，接著聽見一個聲音從樓上傳來，像是「噓——」。

我抬頭往上看，剛好看見一顆很大的紅色水球。水球上

面是林克的頭，正從二樓的一扇窗戶裡伸出來。

水球在我旁邊的階梯上「啪」一聲破掉了。我只有鞋子溼掉。林克大笑還大喊：「給你個驚喜！」接著他說：「肥列克，進來吧，門沒關。」

我的心怦怦跳，幾乎要掉頭跑回家。

可是我沒有。如果林克想把那顆水球丟到我頭上，他大可以那樣做。所以，有進步了，對吧？還是他其實是想讓我全身溼掉，卻沒丟準呢？

無論如何，我進屋了。

林克的媽媽正在前廳檢查一堆信件。她一定是剛剛才回到家，因為她還穿著外套。她微笑著說：「嗨，你一定是傑

克囉，林克說你要過來一起準備報告。如果你們等會餓了，

可以吃點心喔。」

我說：「謝謝你。」

林克從樓梯最上面大喊：「嘿，上來這裡，把你全部的

東西都帶上來。」

林克的房間真令人驚訝。我猜我原本以為他的房間要不

是像洞穴，就會像監牢之類的，結果，只是一個普通的房間。

房間四周有很多漫畫書，所有的架子上都是模型，很多

很多模型。有模型汽車、卡車、摩托車、模型船和飛機，甚

至還有一列模型火車。

我拿起一輛模型車。

「嘿！肥列克，不要摸！」

我把車放下，但還是彎下身子，好看得清楚一點。

模型很完美。這只是一具塑膠模型，就像休閒玩具店裡那種模型一樣，要先用膠水黏好，然後塗成亮藍色。很完美。

我看著林克，他已經跳到床上。他正在看一本《X戰警》漫畫。

我說：「真酷，你怎麼會有這個？」

「我爸給我那組模型，是一九六九年的福特野馬敞篷車。」

我說：「你是說，那是**你自己**拼的？」

「對呀。」林克說，眼光沒有離開那本漫畫書。「也是我自己塗顏色的。」

我可以想像林克會有收集摔角卡那樣的嗜好，或是抓蟲和蜘蛛，甚至是對一面磚牆砸玻璃罐；但是拼模型？林克？

有一個穿綠色T恤和運動褲的女生進了林克的房間。她長得很高，肩膀和手臂很壯，可能是高中生。她每隻耳朵上差不多有六個耳環，咖啡色頭髮前面有一道鮮豔的粉紅色。

而且她很生氣。

她並沒有注意到我，然後用真的非常大的聲音說：「嘿，臭克！」

林克的視線從他的漫畫書往上移。「什麼？」

「你知道我在講什麼。你今天早上從我的衣櫥拿走了三十塊錢。」

「才沒有！」

她拿起我剛才看過的野馬敞篷車模型，把模型舉起來，開始將她的大手收緊。

林克坐起來大叫：「嘿，別動那個！」

她笑了，而那個微笑在我看來非常熟悉。接著她說：「這裡……接住！」然後她把模型丟向林克。

林克在模型打到床之前接住了。

那女孩說：「我知道是**你拿走三十塊**。」

林克說：「你八成把所有的錢都拿去買口紅或一些蠢東西了吧。你這麼笨，可能根本就不記得。」

她往房間內走進兩步。「是喔，好啊，臭克，看看你會不

會記住這點：只要再讓我發現你踏進我房間一**次**，你就死定了。」然後她看著我。「你的笨蛋朋友也一樣！」

接著她離開了。幾秒鐘後，門被重重甩上。

林克露出牙齒對我笑，橫過身來，把模型放在他床邊的桌子上。「那是我發瘋的姊姊。」

我拿出一本書，上面有些美洲原住民村莊的照片，我準備要完成這份報告就回家。我才不覺得超級巨人惡霸女孩很有趣。我說：「我們把事情做完吧，好不好？」

林克無聊的嘆了一口氣。「嗯，好呀，我拿了一些我們可以用的材料。」

他滾下床，走到靠近窗邊的一張桌子。那裡有一個大盒

子，就是那種聖誕節時你會收到的新衣服盒子。他掀開盒蓋。「我們可以在這個盒蓋內面做一個梯皮帳篷。」

我說：「好呀。」

可是我的眼睛看著盒子裡的東西。有一些牛皮紙袋和一些棍子與小樹枝，還有一些裝滿沙子的塑膠袋和幾片乾掉的青苔。有好幾撮長長的綠色松針，以及一些繩子和膠水。

林克說：「這些垃圾大部分是從我家後院收集來的。」

「喔，」我說：「所以你的想法是要讓這個梯皮帳篷看起來像真的一樣？」

他看著我。「廢話。但你想得沒錯，肥列克。」

我撿起一根比較長的棍子。「這可以當做梯皮帳篷的一根

支柱。」

林克搖搖頭。「太粗了，我會用這些細的棍子。如果不用細棍子，看起來會怪怪的。」

接下來一個鐘頭，我看著林克工作。我試著想幫忙，卻只是礙手礙腳的。

林克先選了七根細棍子當做梯皮帳篷的支柱，然後用舊鞋帶的一部分把棍子的一端綁在一起。接著他拿剪刀把一個很大的牛皮紙袋剪開，並解決了如何讓牛皮紙袋恰好蓋住支柱的問題。他在牛皮紙袋上畫滿小小的點，讓梯皮帳篷的篷布看起來像是縫合起來的。

我給林克看我帶來的一本書，他就在梯皮帳篷上畫了鳥

和鹿。他把黑色彩色筆塗擦在紙巾上，然後將紙巾上的顏色擦印在牛皮紙袋上，讓梯皮帳篷看起來舊舊的。接著他把梯皮帳篷黏好，再將完整的帳篷黏在盒蓋上。

他還在帳棚旁邊灑了一些沙子和青苔，並將大石頭放在上面，看起來像塊岩石。他在梯皮帳篷外面擺一圈小石頭，做成一個小火爐，然後用木頭、碎裂的錫箔紙和一枝紅色彩色筆讓火焰看起來像真的一樣。他拿松針做樹木和樹叢，接著又做了另一頂比較小的梯皮帳篷。

真的很神奇，這看起來就像一座小小的村莊，棒透了。

林克放下膠水罐，退後幾步。

我說：「真的很棒。」

林克聳聳肩。「還可以啦。」

我把東西放回書包，穿上外套。「所以你明天會把東西帶到學校吧？」

林克哼了一聲說：「你以為我會讓你帶去嗎？然後看著你走路絆倒，把東西灑得到處都是，像個蠢蛋一樣？我會自己帶過去。」

我說：「好吧，明天見囉。」

林克跳回床上，拿起另一本漫畫。「好呀，再見，肥列克。」然後他說：「嘿，肥列克，你別忘囉，你最好給我好好報告。」

不過那時候我已經往下朝玄關走去。我輕手輕腳的經過

86

他姊姊的房間，然後下樓。我打開門，把頭伸出去，往上看一看。林克不在，也沒有水球，所以我趕快跑過門階衝回家。

有些事我需要想一想。

我在林克家看到了很多事。

像是他的姊姊。一輩子都得和**那樣的人**住在同一間屋子裡，會是什麼感覺？

還有他媽媽。她好像人很好。

接著還有林克。

沒錯，他拿水球砸我，經常不理我，又叫我蠢蛋，可是他似乎不像一個超級霸凌者，至少沒有一直都這樣。偶爾，

他只是……這個嘛……只是像一個小孩。

而且他真的是拼模型的高手。

我看過林克想到模型時的表情，也看過他為模型上色、黏合時的臉。當他忘記我在場的時候，會出現一種和惡霸不同的神情；不凶，甚至是和善的臉。

可是當林克想起我在場的時候，他的臉就會變回來。

所以，如果沒有人可以霸凌的時候，霸凌者就不再是霸凌者了，對吧？

我沒辦法讓我自己消失。

可是我有辦法讓一個超級霸凌者消失嗎？

那是一個我還沒辦法回答的問題。

10 林克破功

第二天早上，林克沒有搭公車。因為要帶報告主題，所以他爸爸開車載他到學校。

早上數學課一過，布萊托太太就說：「我們現在要來看感恩節報告了。你們要先給大家看你們的成果，然後告訴我們為什麼那是最早的感恩節故事的一部分。」

第一組是安琪雅和蘿拉。她們做了一張海報，展示五月

花號的內部情形。海報看起來好像大部分是她們爸媽畫的，而且她們兩個人說話都太小聲，又一直咯咯笑個不停。

接下來是班和卡洛斯展示了普利茅斯之岩，那是清教徒最早上岸的地方。那個岩石是用混凝紙漿製作的，不過他們用的顏料不夠，你還看得到報紙條上的漫畫和新聞標題。不過呢，他們報告得還不錯。

然後，布萊托太太說：「傑克、林克？你們來告訴我們關於美洲原住民的事。」

我說：「我們的報告在走廊的外套架底下。」

林克跟著我到走廊。一個白色塑膠袋罩著我們的報告主題。沙子和石頭讓盒蓋變得很重。我抬起一端，林克抬著另

一端，我們開始往教室門口走。

然後林克停了下來。他的臉看起來很蒼白，嘴唇看起來是藍色的。他用小小的聲音說：「我做不來⋯⋯報告，你知道的，就是對全班同學講話的事。」他吞了一口口水，然後非常輕聲的說：「我沒辦法。」

我們面對面，隔了大約六十公分遠。我抬頭望著他，眼前已經沒有超級霸凌者了，只有一個害怕的小孩，然後我明白為什麼林克一直對我說我必須負責這個報告了。

我突然感覺到一股力量。到了最後，強大又令人畏懼的林克完全臣服在我的腳下！到了最後，輪到我當最最最厲害的超級霸凌者啦！

我大可以這樣說：「噢，坎看！是矮哀叫的小可憐克，海怕報告！」

我大可以這樣說：「所以……你讓我整整一個月怕得半死，現在要我同情你？嘿，狠角色，太糟糕了吧！」

或者我大可以說：「快點呀……我們進教室去，讓全班同學看看了不起的林克‧貝柯斯特吐到地板上到處都是……

哈，哈，哈！」

可是我沒有。

我說：「不會有事的，真的，你只需要站在那裡，用手指著我講到的東西就好。這個模型很棒，每個人都會認為它是最棒的。」

林克用力吞了一口口水，還做了深呼吸。「好吧……不過你會負責報告，對吧？」

我點點頭，我們就把報告拿進教室，放在黑板旁邊的桌子上。

我看著一張我做的卡片說：「我們做了一個東西，呈現美洲原住民在清教徒抵達以前是如何生活的。」

林克把模型上的塑膠袋掀開，教室後面有些小孩站了起來，好看得更清楚。布萊托太太說：「每個人都再靠近一點，這樣你們才看得見，這真的很特別。小心，不要撞到桌子。」

所有小孩都感到很驚訝，我也是，因為我前一天離開他家後，林克又做了更多東西。他做了小小的弓和箭、一些矛

和一些小籃子，籃子裡頭有小小的黃色珠珠，就像是玉米的顏色。

所以我說：「村莊的一部分看起來就是這個樣子，在柱子上蓋著動物的毛皮，就成了梯皮帳篷。」

我繼續講，林克就指著各種東西。他現在看起來不像會吐了。

在講完所有東西以後，我說：「我必須說實話，這整個東西呢，都是林克做的，是他設計的，繪圖上色的部分也是他畫的。我幫了一點點忙，不過真的，是林克做的。」

所有小孩都鼓掌了，布萊托太太也是。林克的臉紅了起來，可是他微笑了。這不是那種霸凌者的微笑，是他真正的

微笑。

那天下午，在回家的公車上，林克坐在我旁邊。但情況不一樣了。他沒有戳我或搶我書包，就只是坐在那裡，像個小孩，和他旁邊一些四年級生開玩笑。

到了我們那一站下車時，我轉向我家，他轉向他家。可是在我走過轉角以前，他大喊：「嘿！」

我嚇到縮了起來。我實在沒辦法控制，那聽起來就像林克那種惡霸的聲音。

他小跑步過來，臉上不是惡霸的表情。他說：「就是你今天在學校做的事啊，謝啦！」他說完後看起來非常尷尬，

然後聳聳肩膀說：「傑克，再見啦。」

我說：「好啊，再見。」

然後我震驚了一下。林克沒有叫我肥列克或肥克。他叫我傑克。

所以現在我四年級了，林克還是住在我家街口轉角。他現在長得更壯了，我想他就快需要刮鬍子了。

我們並沒有變成最好的朋友或是什麼的。他還是覺得我是個呆瓜，我也覺得他還是個笨蛋，我們再也沒有一起準備報告過。

而且林克並沒有停止他的霸凌行為。他只是不再當個超

級霸凌者，而且他從來沒有再欺負過我。一次也沒有。

以我的年紀來說，我的個子還是有點小，仍然是惡霸最好的目標；我看起來還是有點聰明，而且我還是沒有變成狀鬼。不過，現在如果有小孩開始欺負我，都持續不下去。我懂的太多，惡霸沒辦法再耍我。因為在那些惡狠狠的眼睛和那張惡霸的臉孔背後，有另一張臉，一張真正的臉。

只要我繼續尋找那張真正的臉，我就能看見。惡霸知道我看得見那張臉。

然後「砰！」的一下，就像那樣，另一個惡霸破功了。是被我打敗的。傑克・德瑞克，霸凌終結者。

安德魯‧克萊門斯 **13**

Jake Drake
BULLY BUSTER

ANDREW CLEMENTS

Contents

CHAPTER ONE

Bully-Magnet

I'm Jake—Jake Drake. I'm in fourth grade. Which is my best grade so far. I've got a man teacher this year, Mr. Thompson. He's pretty old, but he's not mean. And he likes the same kinds of books I do. Adventure stories, books about volcanoes and jungles and the ocean, joke books, Calvin and Hobbes—stuff like that.

But there is one thing about Mr. Thompson that's weird. Pete was the first to see it. Which

makes sense. Pete is a science kid. He collects bugs and fossils and plants, and he knows all their names, and he's maybe the smartest kid in the school.

After about two weeks of school, Pete pointed at Mr. Thompson. Then he whispered, "He's wearing those pants again."

"Which pants?" I said.

"*Those* pants," Pete said. "The same pants he wore yesterday and the day before and the day before that. I think he wears the same pants *every* day."

"No way," I said. "He probably has a lot of pants that are the same, that's all."

So Pete said, "I'm going to test my theory."

See What I mean ? That's how science kids are.

That afternoon we had read-aloud time on

the rug, and Mr. Thompson sat in a beanbag chair. Pete sat right next to Mr. Thompson and a little behind him. Mr. Thompson started reading, and he got to the part when the Swiss Family Robinson wrecks their ship.

All the other kids were looking at Mr. Thompson's face or at the ceiling or somewhere. I was watching Pete.

Pete pulled his hand out of his pocket. His hand went behind Mr. Thompson's foot, just for a second, and then back to his pocket. And then Pete sat and listened like everyone else.

When reading was over, I got next to Pete and whispered, "What did you do?"

Pete grinned and pulled something out of his pocket. It was a little black marker, the kind that doesn't wash out.

I got behind Mr. Thompson and looked

down. On the right leg of his pants, on the back of the cuff, was a tiny black spot.

So that's how we found out that Mr. Thompson really has two pairs of pants. Every Thursday he wears tan pants that are just like the other pair, but they don't have the little black spot and they look a little newer. Pete's theory is that Thursday must be laundry day at Mr. Thompson's house. Because every Friday, we can see the little spot again.

My best friend is Phil Willis. Everyone calls him Willie. Willie isn't in my class this year. We have gym class and music class and art class together, but for the rest of the time Willie has Mrs. Steele. I'm glad I have Mr. Thompson. I mean, Mrs. Steele is okay, but Willie has a lot more homework than I do. Also,

Mrs. Steele is a spelling nut. And a math nut. And a social studies nut. I guess she's a nut about everything. That's why Willie's favorite class this year is gym.

Like I said, I'm in fourth grade. That means I've been going to school for five years now. And if you count the two years I went to Miss Lulu's Dainty Diaper Day Care Center, plus one year of preschool, then it's more like eight years. Eight years of school.

So here's what I can't figure out. If everybody who works at school is so smart, how come they can't get rid of the bullies? How come when it comes to bullies, kids are mostly on their own?

Because every year, it's the same thing. Bullies.

Here's what I mean. Okay, it was back when I was three. I was at Miss Lulu's Day

Care. It was the middle of the morning on my second day, and I was standing in line for milk and cookies. And this kid with a runny nose and baggy overalls cut right in front of me.

I didn't say anything because I didn't know any better. Remember, I was only three back then. For all I knew, kids with runny nose got to go first.

So I took my cookies and my milk and sat down at a table. Nose Boy sat down across from me. I smiled at him and took a drink of my milk.

And what did he do? He reached over and grabbed both my cookies. Before I could swallow my milk, he took a big slobbery bite from each one. Then he put them back on my napkin. And then he smiled at me.

I looked at the stuff coming out of his nose. Then I looked at my cookies. And then I turned

my head to look for Miss Lulu.

She was still handing out goodies. A crime had taken place, but Miss Lulu was busy.

So I reached over real fast and took *his* cookies. But then I looked down. Nose Boy had already taken a bite out of them, too.

He smiled again, and I could see the crumbs and chocolate ships stuck in his teeth. So I thought to myself, *who needs a snack anyway?* I slid his cookies back across the table, drank the rest of my milk, and went outside to play.

Three minutes later I was on a swing, just trying to get it going. And somebody grabbed the chain. That's right—it was Nose Boy again.

He snuffled a little and said, "Mine." Nose Boy wasn't much of a talker.

Then I said something like, "I got here first." That was a mistake. The first rule of

dealing with a bully is: Never try to tell him why he's wrong. Bullies don't like that.

He yanked hard on the chain and said, "No! Mine!"

I looked around, and Miss Lulu was on the other side of the playground. Then Nose Boy jerked on the chain again, so I got off the swing.

Nose Boy was my first bully. And for the next four years, I was a bully-magnet.

In preschool it was Mike Rada. I called him Destructo. Blocks, LEGOs, Popsicle sticks, crayons, and paper—no matter what I made or what it was made out of, Destructo tore it to bits.

In kindergarten it was Kenny Russell. Kenny was King Bump. There are a lot of times everyday when a bump or a shove can be bad. Like if you're standing next to a puddle at the bus stop. Or when you're drinking a carton of

chocolate milk, or maybe when you're working on a painting. If there was a bumpable moment, King Bump was there, all through kindergarten.

In first grade my main bully was Jack Lerner, also known as The Fist. Jack never actually hit me. He just hit things close to me. Like my lunch bag. Like every day. A big fist does a very bad thing to a Wonder Bread sandwich. And I learned real fast not to bring any little containers of pudding. All during first grade I ate cookie crumbs for dessert.

So that was me. I was Jake Drake, the bully-magnet. It was like all the bullies got together to choose their favorite target. Every bully for miles around seemed to know that I was the perfect kid to pick on. And I think I finally figured out why they all liked me so much.

For one thing, bullies need a kid who's just

the right size. If the kid is too big, then there might be a fight someday. Bullies don't like to fight. And if the kid is too small, then the bullying is too easy. There's no challenge.

Another thing about me that bullies like is that I don't have a big brother, or even a big sister. I just have Abby, and she's two years younger than me. Bullies figure out stuff like that right away.

And bullies can tell that I'm not the kind of kid who runs to tell the teacher all my problems. Whiny tattletales make bad bully-bait.

Also, I think I look kind of brainy. Most bullies don't seem so smart, and when they see a kid who looks like he is, something inside a bully says, "Oh, yeah? Well, now you've got to deal with *me*, smart guy!"

And I guess I'm a smart guy, because I *am*

good at thinking. And because I'm a good thinker, I finally learned what to do about bullies. But I didn't figure all this out at once. It took me four long years. It took having to deal with Nose Boy, and then Destructo, and King Bump, and The Fist.

It also took being picked on by a Certified, Grade A, SuperBully. Which is what happened back when I was in second grade. That's the year I became Jake Drake, Bully Buster.

CHAPTER TWO

SuperBully

Second grade started out great. My mom and dad had asked for me to be in Mrs. Brattle's class. They told me she was the best teacher at Despres Elementary School. She smiled a lot, and there wasn't any homework, and there was a lot of neat stuff all over her room, so I was happy she was my teacher.

Phil Willis had Mrs. Brattle, too. Willie and

I were already best friends back in second grade, and we had fun every day. We sat at the same group of tables. We were reading partners. We ate lunch together every day, and we always goofed around during recess. We didn't ride the same bus, but afterschool sometimes I went to his house, and sometimes he came over to mine.

Best of all, Mrs. Brattle's class had zero bullies. Not one. It was great. I still had to be careful at lunchtime and out on the playground, but most of the time my life was bully-free.

Then, right before Halloween, a new kid moved to town. The minute he walked into Mrs. Brattle's room, I knew I was in trouble.

Mrs. Brattle said, "Class, we have a new student today. His name is Link Baxter."

She kept talking, and we all looked at the new kid. I could see he was kind of tall for a

second grader. He had blond hair and a pointy nose and long arms with big hands.

Link Baxter stood there and started looking around the room at all of us, too. When he came to me, he stopped. I looked into his face and I saw that Link Baxter had beady little eyes—bully-eyes. And then he smiled at me.

It was not a nice smile.

Then Mrs. Brattle, this lady who was supposed to be such a great teacher, what did she do? She put Link at the same group of desks with me and Willie.

Right away Willie whispered, "Hi. I'm Phil, but really I'm Willie. That's my nickname."

You see, Willie has never had any trouble with bullies, mostly because he's too small. He's a nice kid and he minds his own business, and bullies don't even seem to notice him.

So Link smiled at Willie and said, "Hi."

Then Willie pointed at me and said, "This is Jake."

Link Baxter pointed his beady eyes at me and smiled that bully-smile again. And he said, "Jake. Okay."

I tried to smile and nod at him, but I know I looked kind of spooked, because I *was* spooked. And Link could see I was spooked. And he liked it. And that's when I knew I *was* in big bully-trouble.

Link was only eight years old, just like me. But I could tell right from the start that Link had big plans. He wanted to be the MVP on the Bully All-Star team. He wanted to make it into the Bullies Hall of Fame. And me, Jake Drake, *I* was his new project.

On that first day when Link came to my class,

we practiced handwriting. Mrs. Brattle passed out some lined white paper. We had to write six sentences very, very neatly. Handwriting practice was the only time we could use a pen instead of a pencil.

I loved using my pen. It was made of bright red plastic, and it had black ink. There was a little button on the side. When I pushed the button, the pen went *click*, and the top popped up.

So I was in the middle of my fifth sentence, almost done. My pen was gliding over the smooth paper. My handwriting looked great.

Then Link gave his desk a quick shake. My desk was touching his desk, so my pen went jerking all over. My paper was a mess.

I looked over at Link, and he smiled. Then he whispered, "Nice pen."

So I went up to Mrs. Brattle and got a new

piece of paper. I started copying my sentences again. But now I watched Link all the time to be sure he didn't shake his desk again. I was so nervous that I messed up two more pieces of paper all by myself. And Link didn't make a move.

So I settled down. I was on the very last sentence. Mrs. Brattle was helping a kid at the back of the room. So Link reached over real fast and flicked my ear. Not hard, just enough to make me jump. My pen skidded, and my paper was a mess all over again.

You see, Link was no ordinary bully. Any big kid can push a little kid around. That's one kind of bullying. But this was different. Link Baxter, well... he got inside my head—and it only took him twenty minutes. No doubt about it. This was a bully with real talent.

So there I was, asking Mrs. Brattle for my fifth piece of paper, and she said, "Jake, you should be more careful."

And I almost shouted, "Yeah, well, *you* should pay more attention. Don't you know there's a SuperBully loose in your classroom?"

But of course I didn't say that. Because the second rule about bullies is that if you tattle to the teacher, thing might get a lot worse. And I had a feeling things were going to be bad enough already.

And I was right.

CHAPTER THREE

From Bad to Worse

So I got on the bus after Link's first day of school. I looked out the window. I saw Link walking behind Mrs. Brattle. She was showing him which bus to ride home.

"Please," I whispered. "Not my bus. Not bus three. Please, please, please, not bus three."

But Mrs. Brattle led him right over to bus number three. And ten seconds later, Link was

on my bus, standing there next to me. Looking down at me.

In a voice much louder than it needed to be, he said, "Hey, Fake, anyone else gonna sit here?"

I looked up and I remember how tall he was. But now he was messing with my name. And he already had me mad and scared at the same time. But I didn't care, because I didn't want him to make fun of my name.

So I said, "My name's Jake, Jake Drake."And right away I knew I had made a mistake. Because now he knew that I cared about him goofing around with my name.

Link smiled that special bully-smile. He said, "Yeah, I know. Like I said. Your name's Fake, Fake Drake." And that made the other kids on the bus start laughing. And then he sat

down next to me.

He didn't push me or hit me, because anybody can do that sort of thing. He was a new kind of bully. He was SuperBully.

I felt my ears turning red. My lips were clamped together. I turned my head away from him and looked out the window. I was ready for the next attack.

But it didn't come. A fourth grader in the seat across had a baseball glove. So Link said, "What's the best Little League team in this town?"

And Link started talking about how he was on the top team in his old town. He didn't want to join a new team unless it was going to be a winner.

It was like I wasn't there. I was right there on the seat next to him, but I might as well

have been on the moon.

The bus stopped at Maple Street, and some kids got off. Then at Cross Street, and more kids got off. And then the bus was at my stop, Greenwood Street.

So I said," I have to get off at this stop." About ten kids stood up as the bus slowed down. But Link kept on talking to the fourth grader about Little League.

So I said it louder. "This is my stop. I have to get off here."

I looked over the seat in front of me. There were only three kids left, up by the bus driver.

So I shouted, "NOW. I have to get off NOW!"

The bus driver looked up into her mirror and frowned. But Link smiled at her. And loud enough for everyone to hear, he said, "Oops. Almost forgot, Fake. I'm a new kid, remember?

This is my stop, too. This is where me and Fake Drake get off bus."

Following Link Baxter off the bus? That was one of the worst moments of my life. As I went down those tall black steps, I thought, *Every morning and every afternoon and all day long for the rest of second grade—maybe even for the rest of my life—it's going to be me and Link Baxter.*

Something was going to have to change.

CHAPTER FOUR

Bullyitis

Link didn't talk to me when I got off the bus. He just walked away. I watched him. He crossed Greenwood Street and started to walk down Park Street.

And then I remembered. Of course! Link had moved into the Carsons' old house. The house had been for sale, and now it was Link's house. Right on Park Street. Right around the

corner from me.

When I walked into my house, I didn't even say hi to my mom. I dropped my book bag on the floor. Then I went right to the playroom.

My little sister, Abby, was watching a puppet show on TV. It was her favorite show.

I said, "Give me that!" And I grabbed the remote from her. She frowned at me and stuck her tongue out. Then I changed the channel to *Batman.*

Abby said, "Hey! I'm watching my puppets."

And I said, "Oh, yeah?" And I went over to her. She was sitting on a big pillow on the floor. I felt a lot taller than Abby. I said, "Well, I'm watching *Batman,* and you can't stop me." Then I kicked her pillow.

Abby yelled, "Ow! Ow! That hurt! Mom, Jake stole the remote. And he just kicked me,

HARD!"

Mom came in. She was walking her fast walk. That's her "You're in big trouble" walk.

She stopped and stood over me. She said, "Jake Drake, you know better than to come in here and make a fuss! You come right back to the kitchen and pick up your book bag. And give that remote back to your sister."

I tossed the remote to Abby. By mistake it hit her on the knee. "OWWW!" Now she really yelled, and she tried to cry a little too.

So real quick, I said, "Sorry." But I was too late. Mom took me by the arm and marched me to the kitchen.

She put me on a chair. Then she said, "Jake, we do not treat others like that in this family, and you know it! What's gotten into you!?"

And then it hit me. It was Link. Link had

gotten into me! I was being like Link. I had caught BULLYITIS!

But I couldn't tell my mom about Link. Because my mom might call Link's mom. Then Link would tell every kid on the bus how Fake Drake went and cried to his mommy. And every day on the bus for the rest of my life I would hear about how I'm such a big baby.

So I said, "Sorry, mom." Then I gave a big sigh. "I guess I'm just tired and hungry."

Moms love to hear that. Tired and hungry— that's stuff that moms know how to fix.

Mom patted me on head. Then she fixed me a peanut butter sandwich and a glass of milk. And she said, "I'll make sure you get bed early tonight, sweetheart. But when that sandwich is gone, you have to go apologize to Abby."

So I ate slowly. But then I put my dish and

my glass in the sink and went to look for Abby.

And I thought it was going to be like all the other times I had told Abby I was sorry.

But it wasn't.

CHAPTER FIVE

What Abby Said

Abby was only in kindergarten back then—back when I was in second grade. Even so, Abby wasn't stupid like a lot of little kids are.

I'd never tell her this, but Abby's okay to talk to sometimes. You know, for a sister. I mean, since I don't have a dog or anything. Abby's kind of like a pet who can talk. Sort of like a parrot, I guess.

Anyway, I told Abby I was sorry.

"It's okay." She said.

See what I mean? How Abby's kind of like a pet? You know how if you yell at a dog, it gets all scared of you, or maybe mad? But then you pat it on the head, and it starts wagging its tail again? That's the way Abby is.

She was still watching the puppets. They were painting some clouds on a wall. Really dumb.

Then I told Abby about Link.

And Abby said, "His sister came to school today. Linda Baxter. She's in kindergarten with me. She's a bully, too."

I said, "Really?"

"Yes," said Abby. "Linda took Sara's crayons. I saw."

Abby started moving her arms like the

puppets.

I said, "So she took Sara's crayons?"

Abby nodded, only half listening. "Yes. The best colors. Linda said, 'If you tell, I'll break them.' At snack time Sara gave Linda a Ritz cracker. Then Linda let Sara use the yellow crayon."

So there it was. The Case of Kidnapped Crayons.

And I said to myself, *Linda Baxter is only in kindergarten! Link's baby sister is already a SuperBully.* And then I thought, *Imagine what her big brother is going to do to me!*

Not a good thought.

Abby kept watching the puppets. The show was almost over. The puppets were starting to sing. It's the part of the show that almost makes me throw up.

Then I remembered something. I remembered going to visit Gramma and Grampa in Florida. It was just me and Abby. And I was mad because I always had to do everything with Abby. She was just four. She was still in nursery school, and I was already a big first grader. I hated hanging around with such a baby. I was mean to Abby the whole time.

So I said, "Remember how I was mean to you when we went to Florida?"

Abby was nodding to the music. But she said, "I remember."

And I said, "How come you didn't get mad at me?"

Abby Shrugged. "If I get mad, I feel mean. I don't like to feel mean. So I don't get mad."

Then Abby started to sing along with the puppets. I did not want to throw up, so I went

to my room. I flopped onto my bed so I could think about my problems.

Part of me wished I could get a ride to school with Dad every morning. Then I wouldn't have to ride the bus with Link. And maybe I could go to the library for recess. And then Mom could pick me up after school.

Part of me wished I would grow ten inches in one night. Then tomorrow morning I would get on the bus. I would sit next to Link. I would push his face against the window. I would paint his nose with a red Magic Maker. I would call him Fink. Fink Baxter.

But I kept thinking. And Abby was right. It's not fun to feel mean. Link acted like it *was* fun. But it wasn't really—was it? No. It couldn't be.

As I went to sleep that night, here's what I

said to myself: *Tomorrow, I will not get mad at Link. No matter what. Then he will see that it's not fun to be mean.*

It worked for Abby and me.

But would it work for a SuperBully?

CHAPTER SIX

Playing It Cool

In the morning, Link made sure that he sat next to me on the bus. First thing, he wiped mud from his shoes onto my book bag. But I just smiled and brushed it off. Very cool.

He called me Jake Flake. I laughed and said, "Yeah, that's a good one! Or how about Snake Drake? Or...Cheesecake Drake? Or maybe...maybe, Shaky Jake? Yeah, Shaky

Jake."

Everybody on the bus laughed. But it was me making them laugh, not Link. I was playing it cool.

Link didn't like it. His beady little eyes got meaner and meaner. And when we got to school, he pushed his way up to the front so he got off the bus first. He even pushed some fifth graders.

In class it got worse. Link stuck some gum onto my math workbook. I just smiled and put a piece of paper over the sticky part. I kept working, cool as could be.

During art class Link poured some gold glitter into the paint I was using. I said, "Nice idea!" And I kept painting.

Later, the art teacher said, "Jake, I love what you've done there. Very creative."

Very creative, and very *cool*.

I was worried about recess. The playground is big. Anything can happen out there.

Sure enough, Link cut in line and got behind me on the sliding board. I slid down, and he came down behind me really fast. He tried to bump me into a puddle. But I stepped aside real fast, and his foot went into some mud.

It's a good thing Mrs. Brattle was standing so close. Otherwise, Link might have tried to make me lick that mud off his shoe or something.

After lunch I was in the boy's room washing my hands. I looked in the mirror, and there was Link. Smiling. I tried to smile back, but it was hard. I was scared.

Link kept smiling. He started to wash his hands at the sink next to me. And when I got a paper towel, he cupped his hands and threw a ton of water right at me. Right down the front

of my tan pants. A big brown wet spot.

Then in this baby voice Link said, "Wook, wook! Wittle Jackey had a accident!" A bunch of fourth graders started pointing and laughing.

I tried to laugh, too. I tried to be cool, but I couldn't. I couldn't laugh. Not about that. I got angry. I felt like flames were going to shoot out of my eyes.

And Link saw. He saw me get mad. Then he saw me get even madder about him seeing me get mad. And Link's beady little eyes and his smirky little mouth laughed. At me.

I stayed in the boys' room as long as I could. I rubbed on my pants with paper towels. I fanned my pants with my hands. But when I went back to class, there was still a big dark spot.

And Link had been whispering. Everybody looked at me when I came in the door. My face

turned bright pink. And when I sat down across from Link, he held his nose and made a face.

I couldn't help it. I was so mad. And it made me feel mean. And I lost it. I turned toward Link and I punched him on the shoulder with all my might.

Might is something I don't have a lot of. So I know I didn't really hurt him.

But Link was a lot better at acting than Abby. He grabbed his shoulder and knocked a book off his desk.

"Ahh!" he shouted. "Ahh! My arm, my arm!"

Mrs. Brattle was there in one second flat. "Jake! I am *ashamed* of you!"

Link let his arm flop down like it was broken. He whimpered, "Ahh, my arm! It hurts."

Mrs. Brattle said, "Ted, please help Link down to the nurse's office. And Jake, you come

with me."

As Link left the room, he peeked a look back at me. And he smiled.

Link Baxter was off to get some ice and some friendly words from nurse.

And me? I was off to talk with the principal— probably not a happy little chat. And my pants still had a big stain down the front.

Mrs. Brattle walked me down the hall. On the way, I figured something out. Link was a bigger problem than Abby had ever faced.

This was war, and I was losing. Big time.

Not cool. Not cool at all.

CHAPTER SEVEN

Learning My Lesson

When people are mad at you, they do a lot of pointing. In the office, Mrs. Brattle pointed to a chair. She said, "Wait here." No smiles. Then she went into the principal's office.

A minute later she came out, and so did Mrs. Karp. Mrs. Karp pointed to her office and said, "In there, Jake."

I had never been to the principal's office

before. There was a big gray desk. There was a row of big gray bookcases. And there was a big gray principal. Mrs. Karp had gray shoes, a gray dress, and gray hair. And she was taller than Mrs. Brattle. Even taller than my dad.

She pointed at a gray chair in front of her desk. "Sit there, Jake." So I sat down. Then she said, "You know it's against the rules to hit someone, don't you." It wasn't a question.

And I said, "Yes, I know."

"Then why did you hit Link Baxter?"

This was the tricky part. If I told about Link being a bully, then I would be a tattletale, But if I didn't say *something*, then she would think I was some crazy hitter. So I pointed at the spot on my pants. And I said, "Some water got on my pants in the boy's room. And I thought Link was making fun."

So simple. So true. So easy for Mrs. Karp to understand. And she did. Just like that. She got a friendly look on her face and said, "I understand about feeling embarrassed, Jake. But do you see that hitting is wrong, no matter what?"

And I said, "Yes." Because it was true. I really was sorry I had hit Link. I did not want to have a fight with Link. Ever. For two reasons.

First, because it's not good to hit and kick and scratch and full hair and roll around on the ground. And second, because I knew what would happen to me if I ever *did* get in a fight with Link. I would turn into one huge purple bruise.

So Mrs. Karp sent me back to my classroom. She didn't even call my mom.

As she opened the door to her office for me she said, "I'm sure you've learned your lesson,

haven't you, Jake?"

And I said, "Yes, Mrs. Karp." Only I didn't know if we were talking about the same lesson.

As I walked from the school office toward Mrs. Brattles's room, Link came out of the nurse's office. I think he had been waiting for me. He walked beside me. In the empty hallway Link seemed bigger than ever.

He gave me that bully-smile and said, "Nice move, Flake. Have a good time with the principal?"

This was the first time I had been alone with Link. I was scared, but I said, "It wasn't so bad." We kept walking.

Being alone with Link was different. And I thought that maybe a bully stops being a bully if there aren't some other kids around to watch. I thought that maybe he's only a SuperBully when he has an audience. For a second, it felt like Link

Baxter was just this big kid, and I was walking down the hall with him.

Back then I didn't know as much about bullies as I do now. So I said, "How come you pick on me?"

Wrong question. The SuperBully was back. Link looked at me like I was a bug. He said, "Dumb question." And I thought maybe he was going to push me into a locker or something.

But it was like my question confused him. And just before we got back to room twenty-three, I knew. I knew why he didn't answer the question.

He didn't because he *couldn't*. He couldn't tell me why because he didn't really know.

But there had to be a reason why Link was a bully.

And if I could figure out that reason—or if I

could give him a reason NOT to be a bully—then Link Baxter, SuperBully, would become Link Baxter, *Ex*-SuperBully.

CHAPTER EIGHT

Dangerous Duo

The next week was not fun.

Every chance he got, Link did something mean. Like step on my red pen and break it. Or something embarrassing. Link push me into a bunch of fourth-grade girls in the cafeteria. Or something annoying. Like hide my book bag under the seats at the back of the bus.

I was starting to think that Link was a bully

because Link was a bully. And I was starting to think there was nothing I could do about it. Except live with it. Every day. For the rest of my life.

Just when I was sure things could not get worse, they did. Thanks to Mrs. Brattle.

Thanksgiving was coming, and we all had to do a social studies project about it. Mrs. Brattle planned all the topics. And Mrs. Brattle wanted everyone to work in pairs. And Mrs. Brattle chose the pairs. And one pair was Jake Drake and Link Baxter. We had to do a report to show how the Native Americans had lived.

Link loved it. He thought it was so funny. A big joke.

He said, "Hey, Flake. This is great. It's you and me. We get to make a teepee together. Tell you what. I'll do the tee part, and you can take

care of the pee. Get it? The *pee?*"

I went up to Mrs. Brattle when everyone else went to lunch. I said, "Mrs. Brattle, I don't think I should work with Link on the Thanksgiving project."

She said, "Oh? Why is that?"

"Well," I said, "I just think I'd do better with someone else."

Mrs. Brattle said, " I'm sorry, but everyone else is already paired up, Jake. I'm sure you and Link will do just fine."

On the bus home that day, Link said, "That Thanksgiving thing? You're going to do the report, Flake. I don't do dumb stuff like that."

I said, "What do you mean? We're partners."

Link said, "Yeah, right. And you're the partner who has to do the report."

The next day we had library period. I watched Link. He went right to the reference section. He got the N encyclopedia. *Good*, I thought. *He's going to look up things about the Native Americans.* Link carried the encyclopedia to a table at the back of the library. My partner was working. Looked good to me.

I went to find some other stuff about Native Americans in Massachusetts.

Near the end of the period I went to show Link the books I found.

He looked up and said, "Great job, Flake."

I said, "What did you find?"

And he said, "Take a look." Behind the encyclopedia Link was reading a book of Garfield cartoons. He said, "I love social studies, don't you?"

So there it was: My partner wasn't just a

SuperBully. He was also a moron.

Then it was the day before the project was due.

I had found all the books. I had found all the pictures. I had used my best handwriting to make some labels. I had stuff I could tell about, but we still didn't have a teepee or anything to show the class.

At the end of the day, Mrs. Brattle said, "Remember, all the Thanksgiving projects are due tomorrow."

So after we got off the bus that afternoon, Link came up to me. He said, "Hey, Flake, Did you finish that dumb report yet?"

And I said, "No. We still have to make something to show about the Native Americans."

And he said, "Well, you better finish it tonight."

It was the way he said it. Like he could just order me around. He thought he could just look at me and make me do whatever he wanted me to. But I was tired of doing all the work. It wasn't fair.

Something inside me snapped. And I said, "No. I'm not going to."

Link took a step closer. He said, "What?"

"I said I'm not going to. I don't care what you say or what you do. I'm not going to make a teepee or anything else by myself. And if you don't help, then I guess we're just going to get an F on our report."

Link looked down at me with his beady little bully eyes. He clenched his fists. For a second I thought I had made a big mistake. I was about to get pounded into the sidewalk.

Then suddenly. He shrugged. He said, "Fine.

Okay. Come over to my house about three-thirty. We'll make a stupid teepee or something."

Then he just turned and started walking home.

Standing there in the November sunshine at the corner of Greenwood and Park, I felt like something had changed. It didn't feel like I had killed a dragon or anything.

It was more like back when I wad five. Every night I'd thought there was a monster under my bed. And then one night I'd gotten brave enough to look. And it wasn't there. No monster.

But in forty-five minutes I was going to have to go knock on Link's door. Who would open it?

Would it be my social studies partner?

Or a monster?

CHAPTER NINE

Surprises and Questions

Finding Link's house was no problem. He lived in Jimmy Carson's old house, and I had been there plenty of timed. I had all the stuff for the project in my book bag.

I went up the front steps and rang the doorbell. I heard a sound. From above. Like *shhhh*.

I looked up just in time to see a fat red water balloon. And above the balloon, Link's head,

sticking out of a window on the second floor.

The balloon went *SPLAT* on the steps next to me. Only my shoes got wet. Link laughed and yelled, "Surprise!" Then he said, "Come on in, Flake. Door's open."

My heart was pounding, and I almost turned around and ran for home.

But I didn't. If Link had wanted to put that balloon right on my head, he could have. So that was progress, right? Or was he really trying to soak me, and he just missed?

Anyway, I went inside.

Link's mom was in the front hallway looking through a stack of mail. She must have just gotten home, because her coat was still on. She smiled and said, "Hi, You must be Jake. Link said you were coming over to work on a project. If you get hungry later, you can have a snack."

I said, "Thank you."

Link yelled from the top of the stairs, "Hey! Up here, And bring all your stuff."

Link's room was a surprise. I guess I'd thought it would be like a cave or jail cell or something. It was just a regular room.

There were a lot of comic books around, and there were models on all the shelves. Lots of them. Model cars and trucks and motorcycles. Model ships and airplanes. Even a model train.

I picked up a model of a car.

"Hey! Hands off, Flake."

I put the car down. But I bent over to get a better look.

It was perfect. It was only a plastic model, like the kind at a hobby shop. It had been glued together and then painted bright blue. Perfectly.

I looked at Link. He had flopped onto his

bed. He was looking at an *X-men* comic book.

I said, "This is cool. Where'd you get it?"

"My dad gave me the kit. It's a 1969 Ford Mustang convertible."

I said, "You mean you put it together?"

"Yeah," said Link. He didn't take his eyes off the comic book. "I painted it, too."

I could imagine Link having a hobby like collecting wrestling cards. Or catching bugs and spiders. Or maybe throwing glass bottles against a brick wall. But model building? Link?

A girl wearing sweatpants and a green T-shirt came into Link's room. She was tall, with big shoulders and arms, probably in high school. She had about six earrings in each ear, and her hair was brown with a bright pink streak in the front. And she was mad.

She didn't notice me. Real loud, she said,

"Hey, Stink."

Link looked up from his comic book. "What?"

"You know what. You took a dollar off my dresser this morning."

"Did not!"

She picked up the Mustang model I had been looking at. She held it out, and started to close her big hand around it.

Link sat up and yelled, "Hey, leave that alone."

She smiled, and her smile looked very familiar to me. Then she said, "Here—catch!" and she tossed the model at Link.

Link caught it before it hit the bed.

The girl said, "I *know* you took that dollar."

Link said, "You probably spent all your money on lipstick or something dumb. And you're so stupid, you probably don't even remember."

She took two steps into the room. "Yeah well, see if you can remember this, Stink. If I *ever* find you in my room, you are dead." Then she looked at me. "And that goes for your twerpy little friends, too."

Then she left. A few seconds later, a door slammed. Hard.

Link grinned at me and reached over and put the model on the table by his bed. "That's my demented sister."

I got out the book that had some pictures of a Native American village. I was ready to finish this project and go home. Giant girl SuperBullies are not my idea of fun. I said, "Let's get this done, okay?"

Link heaved a bored sigh. "Yeah, okay. I've got some stuff we can use."

He rolled off the bed and walked to a table

near the window. There was a big box. It was the kind of box you get new clothes in at Christmas. He pulled off the lid. "We can make a teepee on the inside of this lid."

I said, "okay."

But I was looking at the thing in the box. There were some brown paper bags, and some sticks and twigs. There were some plastics bags full of sand, and some piece of dried moss. There were bunches of long green pine needles. And there was some string and some glue.

Link said, "I got most of this junk from my backyard."

"Oh," I said. "So your idea is to make the teepee look real?"

He looked at me. "Duh. Good thinking, Flake."

I picked up one of the longer sticks. "This

could be one of the teepee poles."

Link shook his head. "Too thick. I got these skinny sticks for that. If they're not skinny, it won't look right."

For the next hour I watched Link work. I tried to help, but I just got in the way.

First Link chose seven skinny sticks for the teepee poles, and he tied the ends together with part of an old shoelace. Then he cut open a big brown bag with scissors. He figured out how to make the brown paper fit to cover the poles. He painted little marks all over. They made the teepee cover look like it had been sewn together.

I showed Link one of the books I had brought. Then he painted birds and deer onto the teepee. He rubbed some black marker onto a paper towel. Then he rubbed that onto the brown paper to make the teepee look old. He

glued the teepee together. And then he glued the whole thing in the box lid.

Then he spread around some sand and moss. He used big stones to look like rocks. He made a little fireplace outside the teepee with a ring of pebbles. And he used wood and crumpled foil and a red maker to make the fire look real. He made trees and bushes out of the pine needles. And then he made another smaller teepee.

It was amazing. It looked like a little village. It looked so good.

Link put down the glue bottle and stepped back a few feet.

I said, "It's really great."

Link shrugged. "It's okay."

I put my things back in my book bag and pulled on my coat. "So you'll bring to school

tomorrow?"

Link snorted. "You think I'm going to let you carry it? And trip and fall all over the place like a doofus? I'll bring it"

I said, "Okay. So I'll see you tomorrow."

Link flopped back onto his bed and picked up another comic book. "Yeah. So long, Flake." Then he said, "Hey, don't forget, Flake. You better do a good job giving this report."

But by then I was halfway down the hall. I tiptoed past his big sister's room and went downstairs. I opened the door, stuck my head out, and looked up. No Link, no water balloons. So I scooted across the steps and headed for home.

I had some stuff I needed to think about.

I had seen a lot at Link's house.

Like his big sister. What would it be like to live in the same house with *that* your whole life?

And his mom. She seemed nice.

And then there was Link.

Sure, he water-bombed me, and he ignored me a lot, and he called me a doofus. But he didn't seem like SuperBully, at least not all the time. Once in a while, he was just— well, he was just like a kid.

And he was absolutely a great model builder.

I had looked at Link's face while he was thinking about the model. And while he was painting and gluing. When he forgot I was there, he had a different face from his bully face. Not mean. Almost nice.

But when Link remembered I was there, his face would switch back.

So if there's no one to bully, a bully isn't a bully, right?

I couldn't make myself disappear?

But could I make a SuperBully disappear?

That was the question I still could not answer.

CHAPTER TEN

Busted Link

Link wasn't on the bus the next morning. His dad drove him to school with the project.

Right after math in the morning, Mrs. Brattle said, "Now we are going to look at the Thanksgiving projects. First, you should show what you made, and then why it's part of the Thanksgiving story."

Andrea and Laura went first. They had made

a poster to show the inside of the *Mayflower*. It looked like their parents had done the most of the drawing. And they both talked too soft and giggled a lot.

Then Ben and Carlos showed Plymouth Rock. It was where the Pilgrims had landed. The rock was made of Papier-mâché. Except they didn't use enough paint. You could still see the comics and the headlines on the strips of the newspaper. But it was an okay report.

And then Mrs. Brattle said, "Jake, Link? You're going to tell us something about the Native Americans."

I said, "Our project is out in the hall under the coatrack."

Link followed me out into the hall. There was a white plastic bag covering the project. The sand and rocks made the box lid heavy. I

picked up one end, and Link got the other end. We started toward the door.

Then Link stopped. His face looked pale, and his lips looked blue. In a small voice he said, "I can't do this. Reports. You know, talking to the whole class." He gulped. And then very softly he said, "I can't."

We were face-to-face, about two feet apart. I was looking up at him. No SuperBully in sight. Just a scared kid. And I then I knew why Link had kept telling me that had to give the report.

Then I felt this rush of power. At last, the great and fearsome Link—completely at my mercy! At last, it was my turn to be the bulliest SuperBully of all!

I could have said, "Oh, wook! It's Wittle Winky—afwaid of weport!"

I could have said, "So—you make me feel

terrible for a whole month, and now you want me to feel sorry for you? Well, too bad, tough guy!"

Or I could have said, "Hurry—let's get in the room so the whole class can see mighty Link Baxter throw up all over the floor—ha, ha, ha!"

But I didn't.

I said, "It'll be okay. Really. All you have to do is stand there and point at stuff when I talk about it. This is a great model. Everyone's going to think it's the best."

Link swallowed hard and took a deep breath. "Okay...but you're gonna do the report, right?"

I nodded, and we carried the project into the room and up to the table by the chalkboard.

I looked at a card I had made and said, "We made something to show how the Native Americans lived before the pilgrims came."

And Link pulled the bag off the model. Some kids in the back stood up so they could see it better. And Mrs. Brattle said, "Everyone should come up closer so you can see. This is really special. Careful, don't bump the table."

The kids were blown away. And so was I. Because after I left his house the day before, Link made some more stuff. He made little bows and arrows. He made spears and some little baskets, and the baskets had little yellow beads in them, yellow like the color of corn.

So I said, "This is what part of a village looked like. The teepees were made of poles covered with animal skins."

I kept talking, and Link pointed at things. He didn't look like he was going to be sick anymore.

When I was done telling about everything, I said, "And I have to tell the truth. This whole

thing? Link made it, and planned it, and he did all the painting, too. I helped a little, but really, Link made it."

And the kids all clapped, and so did Mrs. Brattle. Link's face got red, but he smiled. And it wasn't a bully-smile. It was his real smile.

On the bus home that afternoon, Link sat next to me. But it was different. He didn't poke me or grab my book bag. He just sat there. Like a kid. He joked around with some fourth graders.

When we got off at our stop, I turned toward my house and he turned toward his. But before I turned the corner, he called out, "Hey!"

I cringed. I couldn't help it. It sounded like Link's bully-voice.

He trotted over. No bully-face. He said, "What you did at school today? Thanks." Then

he looked embarrassed. He shrugged and said, "See ya later, Jake."

And I said, "Yeah. See ya."

Then it hit me. Link didn't call me Flake, or Fake. He called me Jake.

So now I'm in fourth grade. And Link still lives around the corner from me. He's even bigger now. I think he might start shaving soon.

It's not like we became best friends or anything. He still pretty much thinks I'm a dweeb. And I still pretty much think he's a moron. We never worked on another project together.

And it's not like Link stopped being a bully. But he did stop being a SuperBully. And he never bullied me again. Ever.

I'm still kind of small for my age, still the perfect size for bullying, and I still look kind of

smart, and I haven't turned into a tattletale. But if a kid starts to bully me now, it never lasts. I know too much. Bullies don't fool me anymore. Because back behind those mean eyes and that bully-face, there's another face. A real face.

And if I keep looking for that real face, I see it. And the bully sees me see it.

And *BAM*, just like that, another bully gets busted.

By me. Jake Drake, Bully Buster.